THE
TACKY
BOOK

The authors would like to thank
Mason Delafield and James Parry
for their contributions.

Additional editorial contributions by Robert Lovka
Illustrations by Rick Kraus

Copyright © 1987 by Nicholas Ellison and David Soskin
Illustrations copyright © 1987 by Price Stern Sloan, Inc.
Published by Price Stern Sloan, Inc.
360 North La Cienega Boulevard, Los Angeles, California 90048

ISBN 0-8431-1811-3

THE TACKY BOOK

by David Soskin and Nick Ellison

TABLE OF CONTENTS

*I*NTRODUCTION

Look around . . . is the world coming to an end? Blue jeans are high fashion, feminine deodorant ads are all over television, dumb movies about clumsy axe-murderers are being called "cult classics" and kids are running around with safety pins in their ears. High-tack tackiness is everywhere!

Take heart, gentle reader, things have always been this way. Tacky is as eternal as taxes and neither show signs of slowing down. So what to do? Adapt! Be aware! Take joy in all that is tacky!

Are there standards defining tacky? Of course. Ours! You may want to add your own favorite tackies to our lists (see TACKY TWO), or you may disagree with some of ours. One person's tacky is another's chic. These are our opinions — nothing more, nothing less. If you discover yourself here you might take exception. But we caution you, dear reader, to keep in mind that there is nothing tackier than having no sense of humor!

This splendid little volume is designed to help you filter through the pseudo-tacky in life and revel in the real thing! People, Places, Affairs of Business, Affairs of the Heart — all of them have their proper place in our high-tack society. So settle back in your purple bean-bag chair and surrender to the tastelessness around you. The tackiness you discover may be your own.

I

GREAT MOMENTS IN TACKY HISTORY

History repeats itself...unfortunately. And tacky history is no exception. Yesterday's Nash Rambler is today's Yugoslavian sedan. The mohawk has returned. And those nifty ceramic Buddhas with the clock in the stomach that once adorned television sets now stand ready to offend your VCR. The adaptability of tacky is awe inspiring, but where did it all begin...and why! Here, then, is a Hall of Fame of tacky, a salute to gaudy and garish, a tribute to Great Moments In Tacky History...

NOTABLE EVENTS AND FIRSTS

- Opening of first all-you-can-eat salad bar
- Arrival of Lawrence Welk in America
- Birth of Bob Guccione
- Loan of hairpiece to George Steinbrenner by Howard Cosell
- Gary Hart, Donna Rice and friends sleep on separate yachts in Bimini
- First Miami Beach suffleboard tournament
- Recording of "Oh, My Papa" by Eddie Fisher
- First recording by Barry Manilow
- French Tourist Board's first advertisement of "Friendly France" in the U.S.
- Chuck Barris produces his first game show
- First junior jet set party at a trendy N.Y. disco...Bianca Jagger is there
- Creation of the first backyard barbecue by Attila the Hun
- Brooke Shields declares she's an actress
- Rise of football booster clubs in Oklahoma, Texas and Nebraska
- First wedding catering hall

- Naming of daughter "Chastity" by Sonny & Cher
- First singles weekend held in the Catskills
- First grandmother appears on Price Is Right and declares she is "80 years young"
- First song sung by Wayne Newton
- First poem by Rod McKuen
- First painting by Keene
- Donnie & Marie's first political fundraiser
- Marriage of Jackie and Ari Onassis
- First sermon by Oral Roberts
- First million dollars contributed to the PTL Club
- Spiro Agnew enters politics
- *Gilligan's Island* goes into re-runs
- Self-service gas stations are born
- The first junior high school boy combs his hair in the corridor
- The first shopping mall is built

Inventions Of Note

- Nash Rambler
- Heart-shaped bathtub
- Shopping mall
- Street carnival
- Polyester leisure suit
- Gold chain and diamond pinky ring
- White patent leather loafers
- TV dinner
- Bowling shirt
- Plastic pink flamingo lawn decoration
- Tuna-noodle casserole
- Hairweave/tanning salon
- String tie
- Processed cheese food
- Convertible sofa
- Aluminum Christmas tree
- Designer jeans
- Bowling alley
- Trailer park
- Pocket multi-pen holder
- Time-sharing condominium
- "Baby On Board" sticker

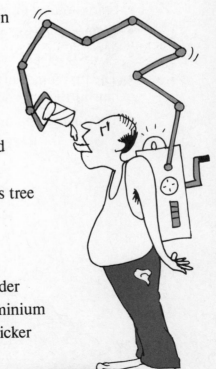

II

LIFESTYLES OF THE TERMINALLY TACKY

For some, tacky begins at home with furnishings like little kitty wall clocks whose eyes rotate back and forth as the tail wags. Or it's found in a bar stocked with wine in twist-cap bottles. For many, tacky is more a personal statement expressed through wearing polyester leisure suits or driving a Cadillac with bull horns on the hood.

Tackiness is woven into the fabric of modern life as tightly as an orange bead in a macramé wall hanging. Here are the patterns. . .

Home Is Where The Tacky Is

- Pink stucco, split-level, tract houses
- Imitation
    - wood walls
    - wood beams
    - wood counters
    - tile floors
    - marble counters
    - brick walls
    - leather chairs
    - flowers and plants
    - poodles
    - fireplaces
- Mediterranean, Early American or catalog furniture. . .all in one room
- Naugahyde recliners, lava lights and fiber-optic fountain lights
- Contact wallpaper, flocked wallpaper, wallpaper with a Saturday morning cartoon theme
- Avocado, aquamarine, rust and gold shag rugs — that meet in the hallway
- Plastic slipcovers

- Waterbeds, round beds, heart-shaped beds, bedroom suites, satin sheets, fur covers
- Motel art, framed centerfolds, black velvet, day-glo anything
- Padded, fur-covered or musical toilet seats
- Wall displays of plates, spoons, trophies, animal heads
- A Vatican souvenir ashtray
- A Buddah clock
- Empire State Building paperweights
- Bronze golf tees as knickknacks
- A stack of old newspapers next to the toilet
- A disco globe hanging in the "wreck room"
- A wreck room
- Chintz or crushed velvet anything
- Wall plaques that read "Home Is Where The Heart Is"

TACKY COMING OUT OF THE CLOSET

- "Designer" jeans
- Terrycloth loungewear
- Leisure suits (particularly green or white)
- Double-knit anything
- Wigs and toupees

- The "Miami Vice" look
- Odor-eaters
- Gauchos and culottes on anybody
- High heels with shorts, cowboy boots, white bucks, white loafers
- Long, glittery earrings with a bathing suit

- More than one gold neck chain
- A Playboy bunny medallion
- More than two rings per hand
- More than two shirt buttons undone
- Nose studs, tattoos, lip and neck stretchers
- String ties, fish ties, naked-lady tie clips, ties tucked into pants
- A plastic shirt-pocket pencil holder that says, "I brake for logarithms."
- Panty lines, any underwear with zippers
- Jewelry that dangles
- Knee-high nylons
- Leopardskin anything

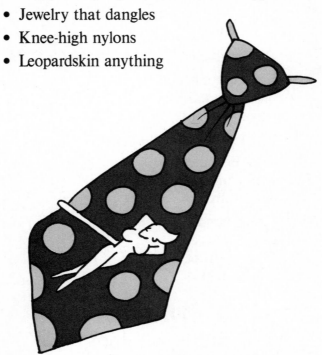

TACKY FOOD IN THE AVOCADO AND HARVEST GOLD KITCHEN

- Processed cheese and anything that looks like cheese but comes out of a ladle
- Crescent rolls, soft white bread
- Canned whole chicken, canned Polish ham, Spam and any other canned meat
- Pour-a-quiche
- Frozen: dinners in plastic containers, pizza, burritos
- Chicken nuggets
- Eggs Benedict with canned deviled ham
- Edible candy underwear (all flavors except strawberry)

Sqeeze Cheeeze!

TACKY BOOZE AT THE WET BAR

- Instant coffee, hot-water cocoa and bullion
- Powdered whiskey sour mix
- Wine in twist-cap bottles

TACKY PARENTING

- Dressing your toddler in nothing but designer clothes from the diapers out
- Bringing a teething 18 month old to a chic restaurant
- Naming your newborn after a natural phenomenon (Rainbow, Moon, Sky)
- Other names on the tacky list are: Buffy, Muffy, Fluffy, Missy, Buster, Sis, Junior, Cookie, Bud and Foxy
- Insisting that your children call you by your first name
- Giving your kids a trust fund and wondering why they lack motivation
- Bragging about their SAT scores
- Entering your three year old in a beauty contest
- Sending your high school grad to a college run by a TV Evangelist

COLLEGE

TACKY TEEN TALK

- Like wow
- Like super
- Like awesome
- Like totally
- Like let's boogie
- Like party animal
- Like groady to the max
- Like barf out city
- Like heavy (accent on the "vy")
- Like go for it, dude
- Like you know
- Like kiss the porcelain goddess
- Like beauty, man

TACKY GOES TO SCHOOL

- Going out for the cheerleading squad
- Going out with the cheerleading squad
- Offering to clean the chalkboard
- Raising your hand to answer every question
- Telling the teacher how much you love this class
- Joining the chess club
- Asking what the homework assignment is when none has been given
- Laughing at all the teacher's jokes

EVERYDAY TACKY

Tacky is as tacky does. How many tacky things do you do every day, every week, every year?

- Celebrating Flag Day and Groundhog's Day
- Going to a boxing match. . .and sitting in the front row
- Going to a porno theater. . .and sitting in the back row
- Hosting a wet T-shirt contest. . .and chilling the seltzer
- Working for the CIA, FBI, IRS or PTA
- Home shopping shows on cable
- Asking stars for autographs, pieces of clothing or money
- Picking teeth in public. . .also, toes, nose or boils
- Taking the "Cosmo Test"
- Participating in a beauty pageant or bowling league
- Watching DYNASTY or DALLAS is tacky. Hurrying home so you won't miss a minute is tackier. Spending the first hour of the next day talking over the plot twists at the office is tackiest!

THE TACKYMOBILE

Get your motor runnin'. . .and put on some tacky wheels.

- Fake fur seat covers
- Plastic Jesus or Magnetic Mary on the dashboard
- Dice, shoes or underwear hanging from the rear-view mirror
- A hula dancing doll bobbing in the rear window
- A "Honk If You Love Jesus" bumper sticker and bunny decal on rear window
- Large words printed on the doors
- Tires larger than the car (or truck)
- One undersized temporary tire
- Barry Manilow 8-track cassettes
- I ♥ anything stickers
- 4-wheel drive off-road cars driven by urban cowboys
- Vanity plates with self-promoting messages — "IMAQT"
- Plastic flowers wired to the antenna
- Stereo speakers suitable for the Hollywood Bowl
- Your car's pet name (JOEY'S REVENGE or BAD GAL NO. 1) stenciled on the rear window
- License plate holders with "funny" messages such as "My other car's a Rolls"
- Brown velour van interiors with rust accents

TACKY HITS THE ROAD

- Signaling a left after you stop for the light
- Blaring stereos playing the latest rap song
- Taking up more than one parking spot
- Letting your burglar alarm blare for hours
- Never looking in the rear-view mirror

THE ANTI-GOURMET GUIDE TO DINING OUT

Everybody needs a little night life. . .try a tacky restaurant.

- Irish pubs owned by Arabs
- All-you-can-eat restaurants
- Any restaurant. .
  - that revolves or is shaped like a boat, car, plane or train
  - that promotes a happy hour, fashion show or fish fry
  - where waiters or waitresses wear theme costumes
  - that uses plastic tablecloths, plastic flowers, plastic grapes or plastic food replicas
  - that shows you your food before it is killed
  - with menus recited by your waiter "Bobby"
  - where cocktails are served with parasols and fruit on toothpicks

Tacky Tourism

- Buying a map of stars' homes (and using it)
- Wearing socks under your sandals
- Referring to the local currency as "funny money"
- Eating in an American fast food restaurant in Paris
- Sneaking pictures at the topless beach

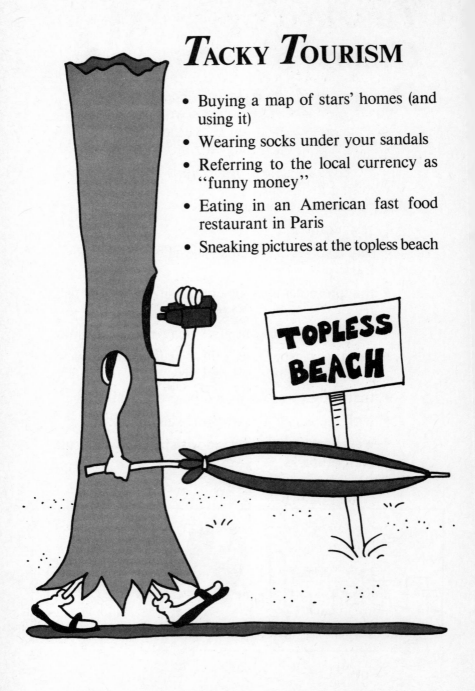

TACKY TRIPS

If you have had your fill of tackiness at home, you might want to break away for a holiday. Of course, you will probably end up in a place that is even tackier than the one you just left! Here are some resorts of last resort that will ensure uninterrupted tackiness:

- Fort Lauderdale or Palm Springs during Spring Break
- Las Vegas
- Atlantic City
- The Bahamas
- The Poconos or The Catskills
- Iran, Libya and Cleveland
- A singles' cruise, weekend or theme trip organized by the local church, temple or travel agent
- Any trip involving a houseboat, RV or trailer park
- Any trip anywhere with a group in matching blazers celebrating satisfied sales quotas
- Any place designed, built, decorated or owned by the Mafia
- Anywhere your Uncle Sid and Aunt Emma might go
- Hollywood
- Religious pilgrimages to ashrams in the northwest
- Time-shares anywhere

III

TACKY RELATIONSHIPS

From the first "I thought I'd drop in and we'd watch TV instead of going out in all that traffic" to the final "You may have really loved me but you never REALLY really loved me" of the divorce, tacky is an integral part of modern relationships. From Meet Market to supermarket to dining alone, the question remains. . .Why bother!?

TACKY AT FIRST SIGHT

- People in a singles bar who:
  - Tell war stories but were never in a war
  - Claim to be 14th degree black belts in Judo
  - End every sentence with, "Ciao," "N'est-ce pas?" or "C'est la vie"
  - Ask you your sign or pretend they already knew it
  - Tell you how incredibly sensitive they are
  - Discuss their work if they are an engineer, accountant or sanitation worker
  - Make repeated remarks about how they used to come to this place with their ex
  - Instantly ask "Do you know what you're doing to your body?" and spend the next twenty minutes lecturing you about smoking and artificial sweeteners

TACKY DATING

Once you actually accept a date with one of these types remember it is clearly tacky behavior to:

- Tell your dinner partner you're going to the rest room and never return to the table, especially if you're meant to pick up the check

- Proposition the waiter or waitress in front of your date

- Suggest a porn flick on the first date

- Return to the singles bar where you met and leave with someone else

THE INVITATION...

- Inviting someone back to your place when all you have at home is a single bed or a waterbed, or worse — a broken waterbed heater in mid-winter

THE MAIN EVENT...

- Falling asleep during it
- Asking "Have you finished yet?"
- Asking if the earth moved after 30 seconds

THE NEXT MORNING

- Assuming your breakfast will be brought to you
- Using the phone to call your spouse ...long distance
- Leaving your business card
- Hanging around

TACKY NUPTIALS

- Theme wedding — i.e., any wedding that takes place while: skydiving, underwater, in a roller rink
- Being married by a mail order minister
- Pledging to "respect each other's space"
- The mother of the bride trying to out-dress the bride
- Having the wedding reception in a restaurant that is open to the public and inviting others to join in
- Any toast that lasts more than seven minutes
- A gift certificate as a wedding gift
- Honeymooning in Cleveland, Niagra Falls, Reno, Disneyland, The Poconos, Las Vegas, Atlantic City
- The mother of the bride or groom gets up and sings along with the band
- Passing out in the limo on the way to the honeymoon suite
- Open bar cut off during dinner
- Ruffled shirt on the groom
- Invitations with a picture of the groom on them

*E*XTRAMARITAL *T*ACKY

- Removing your wedding ring and covering the pale mark with bronzer
- Saying you're separated, when you're not
- Giving any of these reasons why you can't get a divorce:
  - Your disease
  - Your spouse's disease
  - The children's disease
  - Your grandmother's will with the divorce clause

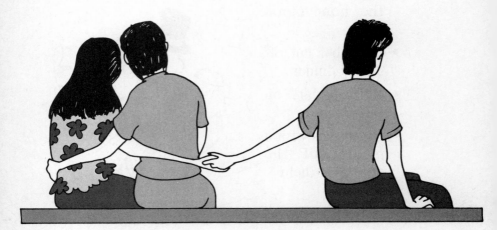

10 *Tacky Ways To Leave Your Lover*

- Get out of the cab on the way to his/her place and send the cab on
- When your lover calls, disguise your voice and say you've left town
- Have your secretary type your lover a goodbye note and send a copy to all of "your" places
- Tell your lover's best friend you've broken up, then seduce the friend so the news will get back
- Ask your lover to return all the things you've ever given him/her — including your picture
- While your lover is out of town, clean all his/her things out of the apartment and change the lock on the door (especially tacky if you've moved into his/her apartment)
- Tell your lover you have another date — but, if he/she wishes, he/she can come along
- Send your lover an announcement of your wedding
- When your lover calls, have your answering service break the news
- Or, hang up the phone cold because your analyst told you to

DIVORCE, TACKY STYLE

- Hiring a lawyer who advertises on TV
- Renting a U-Haul while your spouse is visiting relatives
- Inviting your lover over when you break the news
- Fighting over custody of the dog
- Splitting everything 80–20
- Negating all the good times by saying you were never really in love
- Burning the wedding pictures
- Sending out divorce announcements, even to the local paper
- Having an "I'm free" party and inviting your ex-spouse's best friends

—IV—

TACKY
MEANS BUSINESS

Since the dawn of "upward mobility" and the advent of managers who do it all in one minute, business has been abloom with tackiness.

Now, a new generation of YUTS, Young Urban Tackies, is on the move — mostly in van pools — molding and shaping the tacky practices that will carry business into the twenty-first century. Take a lunch and take a look at some business tackies you know:

TACKY BUSINESS ATTIRE

WOMEN

- Sun dresses
- Slit skirts
- Blue eyeshadow
- Fake eyelashes
- Warm-up suits
- Sequins or beaded sweaters
- Shorts
- Lace anklets with pumps
- Visible petticoats
- Gold or silver shoes
- Huge bows or sweat bands on the head
- More than two earrings per ear
- Strapless anything

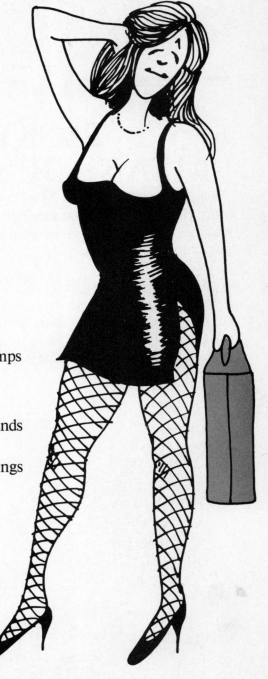

MEN

- Polyester anything
- Chains around the neck
- White socks
- Open silk shirt
- Ankle-length socks
- White shoes, belt, tie
- Purse under arm
- Clip-on tie
- Designer ties with logos
- Pre-folded pocket handkerchief
- Too much hair gel, mousse or hair spray
- Any after-shave you can buy at a drug store

*T*ACKY *B*USINESS *C*ULTURE

- Organization dynamics
- Corporate songs
- Corporate college
- National Secretary's week
- Autographed pictures of anyone
- Pictures of yourself with the president
- "One Minute" anything
- Corporate flags

*L*E *D*ECOR *T*AQUÉ

- "I'm The Boss" sign on desk
- Smoked glass wall
- Linoleum floor
- Metal desk
- Half-dead plant on sill
- Dirty windows
- View of airshaft
- Pin-up calendar
- Gold knickknacks on desk
- Elevator music throughout the office and on the switchboard "hold" button
- A desk the size of Giant Stadium
- Frequent flyer plaques on the wall

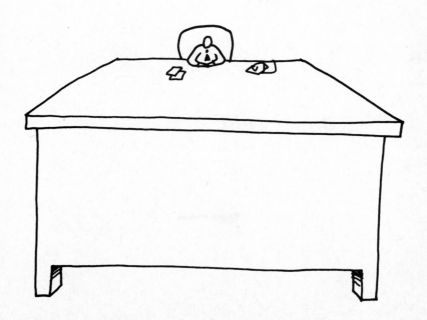

TACKY BUSINESS TRAVEL

ON 4 WHEELS

- Anyone who takes a bus anywhere
- Mini-van car pool
- Pretends the rented limo is his/her own

ON A PLANE

- Talks too much to flight attendants
- Orders a cocktail before noon
- Sends the food back
- Goes to the first class toilet from a coach seat and steals cheese and fruit from the tray

ON THE TRAIN

- Anyone who rides the bar car and has:
  - The same seat each day
  - Plays poker or bridge with the boys on a regular basis
  - Is looking for a date
- Purposely sits next to a friend's 24-year-old daughter pretending to be interested in her new career

TACKY BUSINESS LUGGAGE

- Any hotel or frequent flyer name tag
- Vinyl briefcase
- Metal briefcase
- Designer briefcase
- Any briefcase with corporate name

TACKY TALK

- It's your sandbox
- Viable alternative
- Management will never approve it
- Let's roll up our sleeves
- Thanks for coming in — we'll get back to you
- And I assure you that we plan to let you operate autonomously
- There will be no change in management and you have our full support
- Calling your secretary my girl or my boy
- We need to interface about this
- We'll run it up the flagpole and see who salutes
- Using initials to refer to the boss

*T*ACKY *B*USINESS *P*EOPLE

- George Steinbrenner
- John DeLorean
- Tom Carvel
- Frank Perdue
- George Plimpton

- Barry Diller
- David Begelman
- Avon Ladies
- "Ask Me How To Lose Weight"
- Victor Kiam
- Harry & Leona Helmsley

*T*ACKY *F*IRING

Firing an employee affords the tacky company and the tacky manager unlimited creativity. From Thoughtfully Tacky to Viciously Tacky, dismissal tactics constitute an exciting area in which modern tackiness can thrive. Consider:

THOUGHTFULLY TACKY

The mea culpa cover-up: "Jack, it's possible that the company has failed you as much as you've..." etc. Thus maintaining the fiction that Jack *wasn't* caught embezzling.

The forced retirement party: Where good old Charlie, who has been fired at age 58, is made to endure a retirement party (complete with gold watch and "Charlie, we hate to see you go") and everyone, including Charlie, maintains the fiction that Charlie is leaving voluntarily.

The floor of the forgotten: These include "Mary, we're letting you go" (as if Mary had dearly wanted to go, but, until now, the company wouldn't permit it) and "Outplacement Counseling" (which the company uses to salve its guilty conscience more than to help poor Ernie, who has just been "outplaced").

VICIOUSLY TACKY

Merely vicious tacky: Having a company guard stand watch as Jack cleans out his desk of personal items (of dubious benefit: how can the guard tell if that file folder Jack is taking contains love notes from his secretary — or company secrets?).

More vicious tacky: Not letting Jack go back to his office. (*We'll* go through your desk and send you any personal items.)

Most vicious tacky: Jack comes back from vacation to find that his office lock has been changed.

V

THERE'S NO TACKY LIKE SHOW TACKY

Put on your sequined sunglasses, introduce a starry-eyed Midwesterner to your casting couch and "Have your agent call my agent" — nowhere is tacky more alive and well than in Show Biz! (Even the phrase SHOW BIZ! is tacky.) Tacky was born backstage, in a trunk, on the road and later turned 50 by trying to play the part of a 25-year-old. Tackiness, thy name is Hollywood . . . . .

PUBLIC IMAGE
NUMBER ONE

- Doing anti-drug TV ads while stoned
- Never leaving home without five of the biggest Neanderthals alive as bodyguards
- Refusing to attend the Academy Awards for political reasons

TACKY SHOW FOLK

- Sean Penn
- Eric Estrada
- Britt Ekland
- Wayne Newton
- Sonny Bono
- Red Buttons
- Vanna White
- Regis Philbin
- Merv Griffin
- Richard Dawson
- He-Man
- Geraldo Rivera
- Joe Franklin
- Florence Henderson
- Jerry Falwell
- The Smurfs
- John Travolta
- Pia Zadora
- Pat Boone
- Debbie Boone
- Barry Manilow
- Joan Collins (especially when she's in the middle of a divorce)

THE TACKY
WALK OF FAME
CHARTER MEMBER
— Tiny Tim

*T*ACKY
*T*WOSOMES

- Hugh Hefner and anyone
- Rod Stewart and anyone
- Cher and anyone
- Steve and Edie
- Mick Jaggar and Jerry Hall

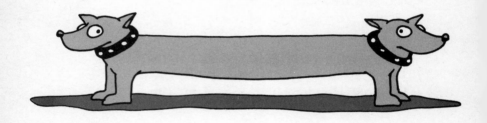

- Donnie and Marie
- John and Bo
- The Captain and Tenille
- Jim and Tammy Faye Bakker
- Sylvester Stallone and Brigitte Neilson
- Dolly Parton

VI

TACKY THROUGH THE YEAR

Each year affords you the possibility of 365 truly tacky days, some of which may easily become tacky through no fault of your own. Also, there are rituals and revelries that were simply born tacky and there's not much you can do to salvage them . . .or their practitioners. Herewith a calendar for twelve months of tastelessness!

NEW YEAR'S

- Spending $1,000 a couple at a "swank" restaurant or club
- Dressing up as Father Time or Baby New Year
- Wearing a lampshade (classic tacky)
- Throwing up in Times Square

VALENTINE'S DAY

- Asking your secretary to buy a present for your spouse
- Giving a woman a huge, red satin box full of cheap candy
- Giving a man boxer shorts covered with red hearts

ST. PATRICK'S DAY

- Showing everyone your green tongue
- Wearing a "Kiss me, I'm Irish" button that flashes
- Using the day as an excuse to fondle strangers

EASTER

- Marching in an Easter Parade dressed as an egg
- Comic books of "The Greatest Story Ever Told"
- Spending $17.50 to attend an evangelical church pageant complete with a cast of hundreds
- Sending an Easter card to a Jewish friend is tacky. Sending an Easter card with a picture of the cross is tackier. Sending one with Jesus on the cross is tackiest.

PASSOVER

- Spreading grape jelly on the matzo

MOTHER'S DAY

- The tackiest thing to do is forget it

MEMORIAL DAY

- Attending the Indianapolis 500 in any capacity other than as a driver

THE FOURTH OF JULY

- Displaying the largest flag in the neighborhood. . .or any flag one-third the size of your house

YOM KIPPUR

- Explaining to Christian friends that it's "kinda like Jewish Good Friday"

HALLOWEEN

- Using designer sheets to dress your kids as ghosts
- Giving nutritious food as treats
- Giving candy left over from Easter or last Halloween
- Having a theme party for adults and not wearing a costume yourself

THANKSGIVING

- Dining at a franchise restaurant

- Using the day as a reason to say grace even though you don't the rest of the year

HANUKKAH

- Using "Tricky Wick No-Blow" candles on the menorrah
- Buying a six-foot tall "Hanukkah Bush"
- Sending Jewish friends Christmas cards and writing "You know what I mean" on them

CHRISTMAS (this is the big one. . . you've got more chances to be tacky now than at any other time of the year)

- Spelling it X-mas
- Aluminum trees with revolving colored spotlights
- Flocked anything (but you already knew that)
- The computer-generated, photocopied "Look How Successful We Are" annual Christmas letter
- Animated cartoons about "The Meaning Of Christmas" featuring Biblical chipmunks, rabbits and mice
- Leaving the price tag on
- Using the box and wrapping from a very exclusive store on your gifts purchased at the five and dime
- Christmas music by John Denver, The Osmonds, Andy Williams, Glen Campbell or Up With People
- Office parties

VII

TACKY AMERICA

From highway billboards to the pretentiously manicured estates of the nouveau riche, tacky is as American as Route 66. We offer you, herewith, an easy-access tourist map to high spots of low taste!

TACKY IS WHERE YOU FIND IT...
A POLYESTER GUIDE TO THE U.S. of A.

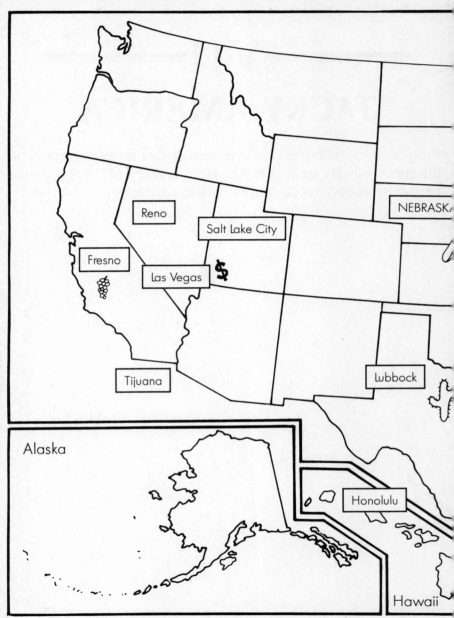

Reno

Salt Lake City

NEBRASKA

Fresno

Las Vegas

Tijuana

Lubbock

Alaska

Honolulu

Hawaii

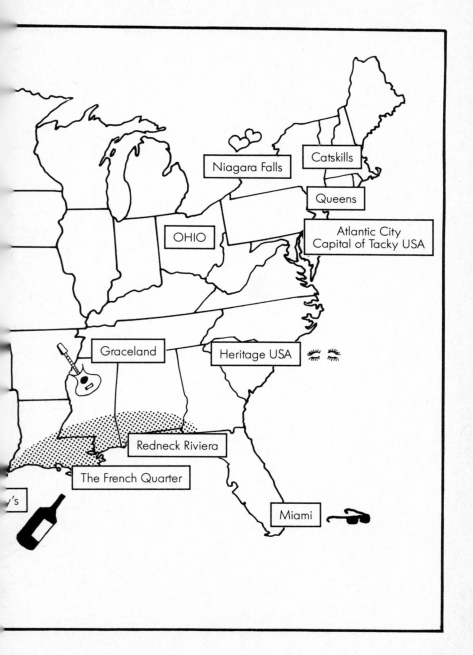

Niagara Falls

Catskills

Queens

OHIO

Atlantic City
Capital of Tacky USA

Graceland

Heritage USA

Redneck Riviera

The French Quarter

y's

Miami

═══VIII═══

TACKY TWO

A FINAL BIT OF TACKINESS

In publishing, it is considered tacky to ask your readers to write books for you, so where better to make such a plea than in this book? Send us your poor, your tired, your disenfranchised examples of tacky and if they're tacky enough they will be included in Volume Two. Never let it be said that we don't practice what we publish.

Send your tackiest little thoughts to:

> *TACKY TWO*
> c/o Price Stern Sloan, Inc.
> 360 North La Cienega Blvd.
> Los Angeles, California 90048

Since it would be something far worse than tacky (it would be expensive) to offer monetary remuneration for the tackies that we use, we will send you a free copy of Volume Two instead. Not too tacky, but it will have to do.

The Publishers

This book is published by

PRICE STERN SLOAN, INC.

whose other hilarious books include:

DEAD SOLID PERFECT
by Dan Jenkins

MURPHY'S LAW BOOKS 1, 2 & 3
by Arthur Bloch

MURPHY'S LAWS OF GOLF
by Ed West

THE CHEAPSKATE'S HANDBOOK
by Mifflin Lowe

and many, many more

The above PSS books and many others can be bought at your local bookstore, or can be ordered directly from the publisher.

PRICE STERN SLOAN, INC.

360 North La Cienega Boulevard, Los Angeles, California 90048